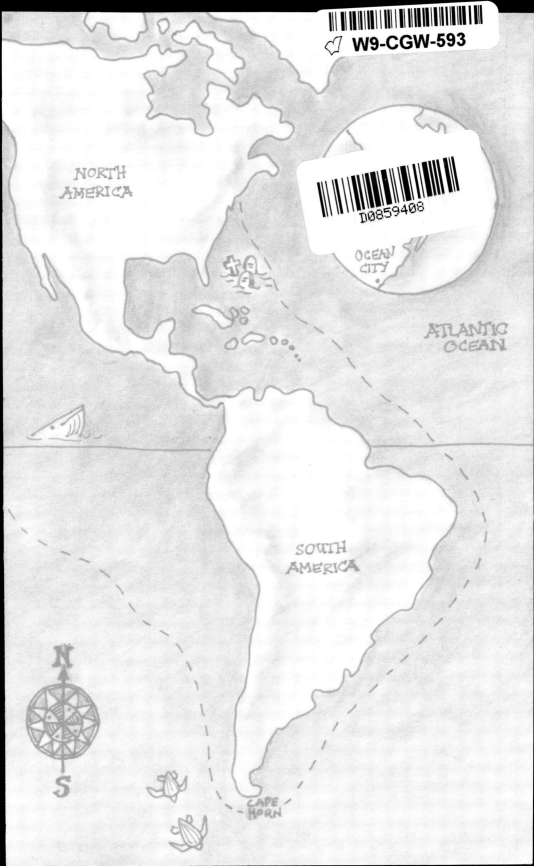

NORTH
AMERICA

ATLANTIC
OCEAN

OCEAN
CITY

SOUTH
AMERICA

N

S

CAPE
HORN

TAKASHI'S VOYAGE

The Wreck of The Sindia

By Lucinda Churchman Hathaway

Text Illustrations by Ellen DiPiazza

For Alice:

Happy Reading!

a bufflehead book

Lucinda Hathaway

8/95

Down The Shore Publishing & The SandPaper

a bufflehead
book

Cover and endpapers illustrations by Leslee Ganss.

DOWN THE SHORE/ SⁿᵈPᴀᴘᴇʀ
PUBLISHING

For information, address:
Down The Shore Publishing, Box 3100, Harvey Cedars, NJ 08008

Down The Shore and The SandPaper, and the respective logos, are registered U.S. Trademarks.
Printed in the United States. First printing, 1995.
10 9 8 7 6 5 4 3 2 1

Library of Congress Cataloging-in-Publication Data
Hathaway, Lucinda Churchman.
    Takashi's Voyage : the wreck of the Sindia / by Lucinda Churchman
    Hathaway ; cover and endpapers illustrations by Leslee Ganss ; text
    illustrations by Ellen DiPiazza.
        p.   cm.
    "A Bufflehead book."
    Summary: In 1901, a twelve-year-old Japanese boy is shanghaied and
    serves as cabinboy aboard the bark Sindia, dealing with homesickness
    and hardships on the long and exciting journey from Kobe, Japan, to
    Ocean City, New Jersey.
    ISBN 0-945582-24-2 (hardcover)
    [1. Sea stories.]   I. DiPiazza, Ellen, ill.   II. Title.
PZ7.H2835Tak   1995
[Fic]--dc20   95-446
                                                               CIP
                                                               AC

Dedicated to Jack, my "true mate."

Acknowledgements

I would like to thank Ellen DiPiazza; Bob Marts of the Ocean City Historical Museum; Ann Wilcox of the Philadelphia Maritime Museum; Connie Mason and Michael Alford of the North Carolina Maritime Museum; Leslee Ganss; Marion Figley, my editor; and Jack Hathaway, my husband. Without their help, I would still be staring at the *Sindia* half-model in the museum, or worse, dueling with my word processor.

Contents

Chapter One

In Dock

Takashi sat on a coil of rope looking out at the bustling harbor. The wind on his face was the same wind that brought the ships sailing into port. Takashi had spent the morning in school. Now it was late afternoon, and he should have been heading home for dinner. Instead, he watched the gulls hover and swoop in the afternoon sky. Their shrill cries seemed to be calling him. *Taka-sh-e-e-e! Taka-sh-e-e-e!* So many gulls meant that a new ship would soon round the point of land which hid the open sea from his view. With the arrival of each ship Takashi's heart rose until his spirits seemed to soar with the sea birds.

Wham! A sudden cuff in the middle of his back sent him flying off his perch and onto the dusty wharf.

"Aiee! Lazy one! So here is where you waste your time, you good-for-nothing!" His Uncle Hiroshi stood over Takashi, brows furrowed and mouth wide, as he continued to voice his anger. Uncle Hiroshi was a very serious and much respected schoolmaster. He thought that Takashi wasted his time and might get into trouble hanging around the dock. Merchant seamen were a rough lot and not good companions for his young nephews.

Takashi rolled over and up in one motion. He bowed deeply to Uncle Hiroshi to show his respect and to hide his face which burned red with embarrassment. Takashi was an obedient boy, but he was angry at Uncle for humiliating him in front of the smirking sailors at the dock. He followed Uncle back to their home as the forgotten gulls continued their song of the sky behind them.

Twelve-year-old Takashi had been looking at the ships tied in dock and at anchor. Kobe was a busy commercial seaport on the Inland Sea, a protected anchorage formed by the islands of Japan. At Kobe's docks, oil from faraway countries was unloaded in big barrels. Japanese pottery, silk fabrics and tea were then loaded on the empty ships for export. Ships from all over the world arrived and embarked every day. Takashi and his older brother, Sami, liked to keep track of the action in the harbor. They would read the ports of call lettered on the sides of the big ships and later locate the foreign cities on Uncle's map at home. London, New York, Genoa, Hong Kong — all had become familiar places.

Since their parents' deaths, Takashi and Sami lived with Aunt Lei and Uncle Hiroshi in a small house near the wharf. Their aunt and uncle had no children and the house was barely large enough to contain them. Sami and Takashi slept in a room that served as Uncle's study. Each morning Aunt Lei stored their sleeping mats behind a screen, and the room became an office. Uncle Hiroshi encouraged the boys to read his books and study the maps and charts that he used in his history classes.

The boys were adventurous, with imaginations that often got them into deep trouble. Takashi was small but very strong and very determined. He could be counted on to do his chores, attend school and work hard at his lessons. His dark hair framed a most animated face that often revealed what he was thinking.

At dinner that evening Sami whispered, "That big four-masted ship is still in dock." Sami was fourteen. In the summer month when school was not in session, he ran errands for a family friend who owned a big warehouse on the wharf. Uncle Hiroshi hoped Sami would learn how to manage a business and forget the sea and his dream of sailing on one of the big ships.

"It's loading and getting ready to sail," Sami continued. "She has been in dock for over a month. I wonder where she's headed?"

"Have you talked to any of the crew?" Takashi asked.

Sami shook his head. The American and English sailors often talked to the boys on the dock and called them "wharf rats." The scruffy, dirty sailors with long hair and earrings were both frightening and fascinating, true exotics to the brothers. The sailors viewed the yellow-skinned, almond-eyed boys with equal curiosity.

Each day brought new ships and new sailors. The harbor was a very exciting place. "A new ship is coming into port. I had to leave before I saw her," Takashi whispered. Once again his mind pictured the deep blue of the harbor. He imagined white sails against the clear sky and the birds fluttering about them.

Later that evening as they unrolled their mats, Takashi said, "After Uncle Hiroshi and Aunt Lei are sleeping, let's go to the dock so I can see the new ship and maybe see what they are loading on the four-master." Sami grinned and nodded in agreement.

Like Sami, Takashi dreamed of adventure, of being on a ship out of the sight of land, of seeing the countries where the red-bearded sailors came from. Much to his aunt and uncle's displeasure, Takashi attended Sunday school classes at the Christian church to learn English. He wanted to be able to talk to the sailors he met at the wharf. The missionaries taught him to understand English, but their God did not replace the Buddha's teachings in his heart.

In the middle of the night with Aunt and Uncle snoring, Takashi and Sami rose silently from their mats. They had to be very quiet in this tiny house with walls as thin as paper. Sliding the doors closed, they paused to be sure that no one had heard them and then ran to the waterfront. It was a beautiful moonlit night.

"The ship is at the dock by Tsumi's warehouse," said Sami. His lowered voice sounded very loud in the stillness of the now-deserted pier where piles of cargo made mazes of shadow in the moonlight.

The boys were wary but not exactly afraid. They were familiar with the dock and had taken nighttime excursions before. Takashi, in his quiet way, was the instigator of these jaunts. He managed to do what he wanted to do and not get into much trouble. Sami, the noisy one, always got caught and often was punished.

"There she is!"

Sami and Takashi stood on the dock staring up at the ship and its gilded figurehead of a brightly painted and turbaned man, his arms held stiffly at his sides and his eyes staring off into space. The figurehead was on the bow of the ship and far above the boys' heads as they gaped at the gigantic face.

"I wonder who he is? Guess he must be a rajah or maybe a genie," observed Takashi. They were amused at the idea of a genie coming out of the bow of a ship. One of their favorite stories in *The Arabian Nights* told that genies came out of bottles.

The ship was as long as the narrow little street where they lived and probably wider. Standing beside it made the boys feel very small. The name painted on the ship was *Sindia*.

"That is a strange name, *Sindia*, I wonder what it means?" Sami whispered loudly. "I wonder where she is going?"

Noises and muffled voices of people approaching the wharf caught their attention. They ducked behind a large pile of crates ready to be loaded on the ship in the morning. As they huddled against the wooden boxes and waited to see what was about to happen, Takashi read the words stenciled in large letters on one of the crates. "New York, New York USA," he whispered.

Sami nudged him with his elbow. Three men carrying an oddly shaped bundle draped in blankets were headed toward the pile of crates where the boys crouched. They were muttering and looking around as if they were afraid of being seen on the dock. Sami and Takashi held their breath when the men turned toward the *Sindia*. As they shuffled awkwardly with their burden to the gangplank, the boys could see a gleaming surface where the blankets did not quite stretch across.

"What is it?" Sami whispered.

"Shh! I don't know," Takashi answered. Now he was scared. Sami and Takashi were both well aware that there were smugglers in port. Valuable religious statues were often taken from the temples and loaded on the foreign ships under the cover of darkness.

These sailors looked suspicious, thought Takashi. As they shifted their lumpy bundle to board the ship, the blanket slipped off the upper part.

Sami gasped. "It's a gold Buddha! Come on, brother! We must get out of here!" Sami jumped up and took off running. Takashi stood up but could not move. He froze in place.

One of the sailors spotted Sami. "Hey there!" he shouted. But Sami had disappeared. The sailor scowled in disgust, turned back to face the crates and saw Takashi, who appeared to be rooted to the edge of the dock.

Takashi's fear paralyzed him. He stood still as strong, hairy arms covered with tattoos grabbed him and a hard, callused hand clamped over his mouth. "Go on!" snarled a mean voice as a rough push shoved Takashi up the gangplank and onto the deck of the *Sindia*.

Chapter Two

On Board

"Look, Captain," said First Mate George Stewart as he dragged Takashi after him into a small room. "This runt was snooping around when we brought the heathen idol aboard. He saw it all for sure. Now what do we do?"

The captain looked at Takashi with absolute disgust.

"What were you doing on the dock at three o'clock in the morning, you scallawag?" he yelled. Captain Allan MacKenzie knew that it was dangerous just trying to smuggle this statue out of Kobe. If the theft were discovered, the ship could be impounded, and he and the crew would land in a Japanese brig. Prisons in Japan were legendary in their reputation for cruelty.

Takashi trembled with fright. His English was not good enough to understand all the captain screamed at him, but it was good enough to know that he was in real trouble.

"Sorry, sir," he said, bowing to the captain first and then to the man called Stewart. Hoping to distract his captors, he added, "I good boy. I good worker."

Captain MacKenzie was a big man, and to Takashi he appeared to be a giant. He had a red beard and a deep, booming voice and looked formidable dressed in his trim captain's jacket with its brass buttons polished and shining. His green eyes narrowed as he stared at the slight, dark-haired boy. Takashi shuddered. He knew that he was in a terrible situation and was not sure what would happen.

MacKenzie continued to scowl and hollered at Stewart for being seen with the stolen Buddha. Just as suddenly, he calmed and his face cleared as if he'd solved a puzzle. "That's it," he said. "I need a cabin boy, and you will be just fine." Turning to Stewart, he ordered, "Lock him in the aft sail locker and post a guard. He shall not leave this ship."

Grabbing Takashi by the arm, Mate Stewart dragged him through the companionway and onto the deck. The ship was noisy with the constant squeaking of the rigging and the dock lines. The quiet port town of Kobe was sleeping, unaware of Takashi's woes on the *Sindia*. Stewart opened the hatch on a sail locker on deck. He shoved Takashi inside and slammed the hatch. The locker was dark and damp and smelly. Takashi was trying hard to be brave, but he cried silently. He didn't want that dirty sailor to know he was scared. He could feel the rough canvas of the heavy sails stacked around him. With the hatch closed and fastened, he was trapped. The scared boy huddled against the canvas, wrapped his arms around himself and closed his eyes.

Inside the shedlike sail locker, outside noises muffled, Takashi thought about Sami going home without him. How would Sami explain his missing brother and more important, when would he explain to Uncle? Takashi knew that the ship would sail with the tide at daybreak and that he would not be missed until time to head for school. By then the ship would be far out of sight of the Inland Sea, and he would have no way to get home. Tears stinging his eyes again, Takashi rested his head on his arm.

The sail locker hatch door flew open. "Out!" ordered a rather quiet voice. Takashi crawled out of the locker and saw a boy barely older but much larger than himself. "The captain wants to see you in his cabin. How did they get you? Can you speak the king's English?" the boy asked.

The stream of questions poured over Takashi so quickly that he could understand only a few words. Still, he felt a little hopeful at the sight of a sailor nearer his age. The boy leading Takashi across the deck was at least ten inches taller and many pounds heavier than he. Dressed in sailor's shirt and pants with a marlinspike stuck in his heavy brown leather belt, he looked like a full-grown man, but when he spoke to Takashi it was evident that he was still a boy. His hair was a tangle of red curls that his mother would have known had not been combed for days, nor washed, and neither had he.

Takashi blinked and squinted in the daylight and felt a new motion of the ship. It was morning! The *Sindia* had left the dock! Takashi realized that he must have fallen asleep in the locker.

Takashi saw that the square sails were full and heard the whistle of the wind through the rigging. He ran to the rail and looked out over the water. The shoreline was shrinking; as it grew smaller, the lump in Takashi's throat grew larger and larger. He was sailing away from Japan and his family! Sami probably had watched from afar when he had been shoved up the gangplank. Although Takashi was scared, he felt sorry for Sami. He knew that Uncle Hiroshi would surely scream at Sami when he was told the story. Takashi could imagine that Uncle would tell Sami that his brother would die on that godless ship. Gentle Aunt Lei would listen to the shouting and cry. Takashi had always wanted to sail away on one of the big four-masters. Being on the *Sindia* was a dream come true, but in his dream Takashi had never been frightened. Now he was.

"Come on, the captain's waiting," said the boy as he grabbed Takashi's arm.

"Where we go?" asked Takashi.

"We're bound for New York," answered the boy.

"What day is it?" Takashi asked.

"It's July 8, 1901, my fourteenth birthday. Now, come on!"

Chapter Three

A Job for Tashi

"What's yer name?"

"Takashi," answered Takashi, stumbling to keep up with the young sailor.

"Tashi? Funny name! My name's Charley."

"Hello, Charley," answered Takashi, not bothering to correct the other boy's pronunciation of his name.

Charley led Tashi to the stern of the big ship. Aft of the

wheel was the captain's private quarters, a small houselike structure built high enough to overlook the working deck of the ship. Overhead, the sails were rounded and full of wind. The only sound was the singing vibration of the halyards and the rush of the ship through the waves. Charley opened a door and practically dragged Tashi through. "Here he is, Captain. Says his name is 'Tashi.'"

"Front and center," growled Captain MacKenzie. "Off with you," he ordered Charley. In the light of day, Tashi could see that the captain's quarters were quite luxurious. Shiny brass oil lamps lighted the cabin. Tashi could see the captain's unmade bunk through a door aft of the navigation table where the captain stood as he rolled up a large paper chart. Captain MacKenzie ignored Tashi and concentrated on the rolls of paper stacked on the table. Finally, he looked at the boy. "What am I to do with you?" he said. He was puffing on a pipe and patting a big black dog. Over his head hung a fancy bamboo cage with a canary singing and chirping. The captain really did not look any sterner than Uncle Hiroshi did at times. "Tashi, that your name? Do you like animals?"

Tashi took a deep breath and answered, "Yes, I like animals." At that moment he looked down. A little calico cat was rubbing up against his legs and purring.

"I can see that animals like you. Old Chauncey never gets near to anyone," said Captain MacKenzie, grinning suddenly. His white teeth showed through his red whiskers.

Tashi scooped up Chauncey and hugged the cat close. He felt better just soaking in the warmth and the vibrating purr.

"You will take care of my animals and the bird," said the captain. "Drake," he said pointing to the dog, "has sailed round the world with me for three years. I just picked up this canary in Japan to take home to my wife. Need to think of a name for it."

"My bird name Lee," whispered Tashi who was feeling less scared with Chauncey purring in his arms.

"That's as good a name as any," said Captain MacKenzie. "Lee, it is! Now sing, bird!" He tapped his finger on the cage, turned to Tashi and bellowed, "This cabin needs to be cleaned! You will do what any of the officers says needs doing, including washing clothes and polishing boots!" Tashi forgot to be afraid as he listened to the captain's orders.

"Charley! Charley! On the double!" the captain boomed. Charley appeared through the door in an instant. "Show Tashi the ship! Find him some gear and bring him back. You are no longer my cabin boy. Report to Cookie when you're finished. You will assist in the galley." A big grin spread over Charley's face. Working in the galley meant that he was now an able-bodied seaman, and he would learn to set sail and work the ship.

Charley and Tashi walked the deck from stem to stern. Tashi could not keep track of the number of men aboard the ship. There were many, thirty or more, and everyone on deck seemed to be working. Men were sewing sails, swabbing the deck, polishing lamps and, aloft in the rigging, tying sails. High above the sails, a sailor in the crow's nest scanned the horizon with a watch glass. Mate Stewart was at the wheel steering the ship. He was talking with a man who was holding a megaphone, ready to relay orders to the busy crew.

Tashi's eyes could not move fast enough to see everything that was happening. Mate Stewart ordered a sail change and ten men scrambled up the ratlines and out on the yards to set the new sails. They moved together and balanced their feet on the lines that ran along the underside of the yards. When the sails were set, the men appeared to dance their way back to the deck. The whole performance reminded Tashi of the Chinese high-wire acrobats he had seen the summer before in the open square in Kobe.

The ship was wonderful. It had four masts and sails that billowed full as they moved along. The smell of camphor oil spilled on the deck was very strong. Tashi recognized the smell from all of the barrels of oil stacked in Tsumi's warehouse. Camphor oil must be part of the cargo, he thought.

"You hungry?" asked Charley as they approached another small structure on the deck.

"Hi, Cookie," said Charley as they entered the cookhouse. "Looks like you're going to have a new helper."

"Who's gonna help me? That little runt?" snorted the cook. He stood with his hands on his hips as he observed the two boys.

Tashi tried not to stare at the cook, a short, stocky man with a green scarf tied around his head covering long, scraggly hair. In his right ear gleamed a gold earring, and there was a nasty scar on his forearm that looked as if the arm had been cut off and sewed back on.

"No, not him, Cookie. Me," laughed Charley.

"Oh — you. Well, I guess that's better than nothing, which is what I got now. Who's the runt?" asked Cookie.

"This is Tashi, and he's hungry," said Charley.

"He looks like he needs a good meal. Don't know if he'll get one on this old tub," muttered Cookie as he poured Charley and Tashi mugs of tea. "There's some bread and 'lasses. Help y'self." Charley cut a big hunk of bread from the loaf on the table and dug out some molasses from a sticky jug to spread on it. "Watcha waitin' for?" Cookie asked Tashi.

"What is this? Is there rice?" murmured Tashi. He looked at the bread and brown goo in wonder. Tashi was used to vegetables and rice. This was an awful, smelly mess.

Cookie understood at once and said, "Only has rice twice a week, and today ain't it." He smeared a piece of bread with molasses and handed it to Tashi. "Eat!" he commanded.

Tashi's nose objected to the smell of the molasses as he looked suspiciously at the food and ate.

After the tea and the bread, Tashi did feel a little better. He had never tasted anything like these foods, and he wasn't sure that he wanted to ever again.

The galley was dark and dirty. The stove behind Cookie was smoking and covered with spills and food crumbs that made Tashi long for Aunt Lei's tidy house that he had left behind in Kobe. Cookie was a tough-looking man, but as Tashi handed him the mug, he reached out and touched Tashi's shoulder in a very comforting way.

"Now, you stick with Charley. He knows the ropes. If yer ever hungry, come in. We has rice on Tuesday and Friday. I'll save you some extra," said Cookie.

Tashi left the kitchen feeling that Cookie was a friend, but he was still too scared to be sure about Charley who was leading him out of the cookhouse. He followed Charley into the gloom belowdecks to the foc'sle area where the sailors had their bunks and hammocks. What a sight it was! Snoring, sleeping men sprawled in some of the bunks, with drying clothes strung everywhere. The smell of the sweaty, dirty sailors snoring away in the cramped space made Tashi feel a little sick. Then and there, Tashi decided that the only way he'd want to sail was as the captain of a ship.

Because of the rotating watches, there were always men on deck and men awake and men asleep. For the crew, life and the schedule on ship began and ended every four hours.

From the foc'sle, Charley opened a hatch and headed down a ladder deeper into the hold of the ship. There were barrels of camphor oil, tatsumi mats and crates of all sizes fastened down so they wouldn't shift around in rough weather. Charley told Tashi that most of the cargo was Japanese silks and porcelain vases and dishes. He said they were all colors and shapes and would sell for a lot of money in New York City.

Suddenly a rat scampered out from behind a stack of crates in front of the boys.

"Pesky things. Real ugly and hard to catch," said Charley. "All us seamen has to keep after 'em because they get into the food. If we keep 'em out of that, they chew on the sails and ropes. You'll be catchin' your share and tossing 'em overboard," he said matter-of-factly.

Even as Tashi listened to Charley, his eyes searched the dark hold. Tashi knew that the Buddha was somewhere nearby, but he did not like being so far under the water in the hold of the ship. He could not see the Buddha and imagined that it must have been hidden in the midst of the cargo. Having the Buddha aboard made Tashi know that he could survive the smells, the rats, the hard work and the uncertainty of his future. What was to happen? Buddha's presence was comforting, but knowing that a rat could appear at any moment was not.

"Let's go topside. You've seen all of her," announced Charley.

"Big ship and many men," was all that Tashi could voice.

It was time for the older boy to report to his new duties in the galley, and it was time for Tashi to go back to the captain. The day was beautiful, and the ship almost seemed to sail herself while the men watched and worked. This was the sort of day that captured seamen forever: sun, wind, a new voyage and dreams of adventure. Tashi entered the captain's quarters.

Chapter Four

On Course

Captain MacKenzie was standing at the navigation table when Tashi timidly entered the cabin. "Well, what do you think of her?" he boomed at Tashi. "The *Sindia's* a fine ship, and it's a good crew." The captain seldom waited for anyone to answer him; he just kept right on talking. "She's a bark, three hundred twenty-nine feet long. We are sailing for New York round Cape Horn. We should be in New York by Christmas. The ship is full of pottery and silk for the Christmas trade."

All the time he spoke, the captain drew lines on the map and scribbled numbers. "Come over here," he ordered Tashi. "This is the Pacific Ocean," he said, pointing to a huge chart spread on the table. "Aboard ship all maps are called charts.

"Here's Kobe, your home port, and here's Cape Horn. We will sail straight on till we get there," said the captain, tracing the route with his finger and never really looking at Tashi.

Tashi did not understand everything the captain said, but he was familiar with charts and navigation because he had studied maps and charts in school. Tashi's father had been in the Japanese navy, and Uncle Hiroshi used to tell tales of his brother's early sailing trip to China. Tashi peered at the chart spread out on the table and followed the course that the captain had set. They were to cross the whole Pacific Ocean and round the tip of South America, sail into the Atlantic Ocean and north to New York City. It was a long voyage. Tashi wondered how he would ever return to Japan and his family, but he was excited with the chance to sail halfway round the world. The circumstances of Tashi's being dragged aboard the ship were not mentioned by the captain and, for the moment, they were forgotten by Tashi, too.

The captain kept drawing lines and making notes as Tashi watched. Then he stopped, looked at Tashi and barked, "Get to work, you scallawag!"

"What I do?" asked Tashi, startled by the sudden, booming voice.

"Get this cabin cleaned up and then bring me a cup of tea! Quick now!" At that moment the ship's clock sounded eight bells. "That's the changing of the watch. I'm going on deck. Bring my tea to me there when you've cleaned up," commanded the captain.

The cabin was a mess, all but the chart table which stood in the center, in perfect order. Around the table were bundles and packages that had been tossed into the room and ignored. Aft was the captain's bunk and shaving basin. Tashi smoothed the white sheets on the bunk. He cleaned up the morning shaving gear, gathered all of the dirty linens and stowed away the captain's gear from the chart room. The birdcage needed his attention, and Drake's head needed to be scratched. It was really an easy job, and Tashi didn't waste any time. He was soon ready to get the tea.

Tashi left the captain's quarters and walked across the deck to the cookhouse. Cookie and Charley seemed glad to see him. "Tea for Captain MacKenzie," said Tashi.

"Don't spill any," warned Charley as he handed Tashi a mug that was big at the bottom and small at the top. Tashi took the mug and walked to the bridge where Captain

MacKenzie was in charge. He quietly handed the tea to the captain and then he watched.

George Stewart was at the helm. The wind was behind the *Sindia* so all sails were full. Huge square sails on the three forward masts and the triangular spanker of the fourth mast were driving the ship forward, hard and smooth. With the wind in his face and the salt spray on his lips, Tashi thought that this must be what the gulls feel as they soar on the wind. The white sails framed by blue sea and sky were a beautiful sight.

"We're sailing our proper course, Cap'n. It's a fair wind," said Stewart.

"Hold this course and steady as she goes. We will check the course in one hour," replied the captain.

"Aye, aye, sir," said the mate.

The captain walked forward to look over the ship, and the mate gave the wheel to a seaman while he checked the charts. Able-bodied seamen could steer the ship, but the captain and

 the first mate navigated and made the decisions. The seamen just maintained the course by steering the ship and keeping the

compass heading exactly where they were told. If the wind changed direction, the officer in charge decided what course to steer and which sails to set and issued the orders.

It was fast getting dark, and Tashi's stomach gave a rumble. He wondered when and where he would eat, but having two friends in the cookhouse made him feel confident that he would not be hungry.

The captain walked by and handed Tashi his mug. "Come with me," he said, and Tashi followed him back to his quarters.

The captain pointed to a dark corner in the companionway, the corridor just outside his cabin. "That's where you'll bunk so I can call you if I need you. Get a bedroll out of that chest." The captain pointed to a small chest attached to the deck in the rear of the companionway. "That'll be where you stow your gear."

The captain then opened the door directly across from the chart room and his bunk. "Come in," he called. "This is the saloon where the officers eat. You'll eat after us."

Sleeping in the companionway outside the captain's quarters would be warm, and eating after the officers would be just fine with Tashi. He was feeling pretty good.

"I don't stand watch and neither will you," said the captain to Tashi. "The rest of the crew is divided into two watches, the starboard watch and the port watch. You'll soon see how it works."

Bells rang. Tashi didn't count, but the captain said, "Six bells. That'll be supper. Help Charley if you can." Tashi turned to go just as Charley hurried in, carrying a tray of food.

Tashi helped Charley put the food on the table: boiled potatoes, dried beef, biscuits and coffee. Charley set some pudding on the side for dessert. None of the food was familiar to Tashi, but the new smells made his mouth water with hunger.

George Stewart and Second Mate George Wilkie entered the saloon and sat at the table with the captain and the other officers. They ate their dinner in silence. The captain had talked to Tashi more that afternoon than he did to the men at dinner. Drake begged for crumbs, and the captain fed him under the table. Chauncey was more aloof and must have known that the captain would get up from the table and bring him some food. The men finished eating, lit their pipes, sat back and began to discuss the day's voyage. Tashi cleared the table, ate what he wanted and took the dishes to the cookhouse. The dried beef's salty taste was still in his mouth. He decided that the biscuits were pretty good, and he had licked every bit of pudding from the bowl. There was enough food to keep him from going hungry.

The first day at sea had been a long one. Tashi was ready to sleep that night. He wondered what new adventure tomorrow would bring.

Chapter Five

King Neptune's Greetings

The *Sindia* was making great progress sailing through the Pacific Ocean. Two months passed without going ashore. Often the seaman on watch in the crow's nest would call out, "Ship to starboard!" or "Ship to port!" but the ship would be too far away for the crew to see from the deck.

Tashi lived in the captain's deckhouse and ate from the captain's table which set him apart from the crew but did not keep him from making friends. Over the long weeks, he and Charley became mates, true friends. They helped each other and shared the secrets of their lives. Charley was quickly learning to be an able-bodied seaman and what he learned he soon taught to Tashi when the two boys talked, Charley chattering away in English, Tashi speaking slowly and carefully.

Time now had a different meaning for Tashi. When he checked the captain's log, he was surprised to see that two months had gone by since they had set sail. Two months out of sight of land, away from his family, eating strange food, learning a new language and living his dream of sailing. The rhythm of the sea had taken over: morning and night, stars and sun, constant splash of the bow as the *Sindia* cut through the waves. The sky connected Tashi to his home. He knew it was the same sky over Kobe and that Sami was looking at the same sun. This very sun that was guiding the *Sindia* was in the center of the Japanese flag flying over the harbor in Kobe.

John Hand, the ship's carpenter, took a liking to Tashi. John showed him how to use the lathes and planes that smoothed the wood and sometimes let Tashi practice his skill. John and his precious tools held the ship together. He repaired whatever was broken, and his job was never-ending. Tashi wanted to make a half model of the *Sindia* to take with him when he left the ship. In the museum in Kobe, the half models Tashi had seen looked like miniature ships that had been sliced in two from stem to stern. These models were replicas of many famous sailing ships. Tashi wanted to make one of his ship.

One day John showed Tashi the plans of the *Sindia*. The true measurements of the ship were on the plans.

"Could I make half model of the *Sindia*?" Tashi asked John. The carpenter thought about it, cocking his head to one side and looking at Tashi.

He smiled and answered, "I suppose, but you'd have to keep me in tea and 'lasses for as long as it took."

That was easy. Tashi knew that Charley would allow him to have tea and molasses for John whenever he wanted. John and Tashi looked around for scraps of mahogany left over from repairs to start building the half model.

It was a difficult project for a young boy, but John was a patient teacher. He was a quiet man who kept to himself but who was always ready to eat or to have fun. Tashi was fascinated by the leather apron that the carpenter wore. It had many pockets full of tools and bits and pieces that he used in his work. The apron stretched tightly around John's middle. He was the fattest man aboard, but he could still scramble up the rigging with the rest of the crew.

As ship's carpenter, John did have to stand watch but went aloft only in an emergency. The watches began at eight o'clock at night and changed every four hours until breakfast time when the routine of the day began again.

Every day was the same, with wonderful breezes and shining sun on the broad, blue sea. Only Sunday was different when Captain MacKenzie read to his crew from the Bible, a practice common on sailing ships, Charley told Tashi. The Bible admonished that Sunday was to be a day of rest, but whittling or carving for pleasure was not considered work, and the men enjoyed their Sunday afternoons. One Sunday, John and Tashi had just settled themselves to an afternoon of carving on the half model when a loud voice interrupted them.

"You making a wooden shoe?" Seaman Anthony Briggs teased Tashi, looking over the boy's shoulder. Tashi looked up from the block of mahogany with a pointed end that he was patiently shaping.

"What a waste of time on this beautiful day. Come on, I'll teach you to play the accordion," Briggs said, laughing. He walked to the foredeck where a group of men were singing and talking.

Tashi wondered why Briggs was always sticking his nose into everyone's business. He was the only sailor aboard who was usually grumpy and complaining. John Hand had told Tashi that when Briggs was ashore he was happy. He was young and strong and was usually surrounded by pretty girls. This would probably be his last voyage. Briggs was repeatedly telling everyone how many days were left till they reached New York.

Tashi gave Briggs a quick, nervous smile and ducked his head. He pretended not to understand and continued to plane the wood. "John, you think it close to the right shape?" he asked the carpenter.

Taking the model in hand, John looked and ran his fingers up and down the smooth side. "You're getting there. Keep planing and carve a little out of this side," he added, pointing to one end.

There had been lots of talk aboard the ship that they would soon "cross the line" at the equator as the *Sindia* sailed south. Charley had told Tashi that crossing the equator called for a celebration. Tashi had been keeping his eye on the chart in the captain's quarters and knew that they were getting close. He watched the sea birds following in the wake of the ship, felt the warm breezes on his face, thought of Sami and wished he could tell him about this voyage. All the while he worked on the model. It was an almost perfect day.

Suddenly, cold water drenched Tashi. Water poured over his head as John Hand danced in front of him with a mop on his head. Seamen were everywhere, singing and dancing and throwing water on Tashi. Even the captain was there, laughing and watching the men cavort and dance around the deck. They are all crazy, thought Tashi, clutching his model and looking wildly about him.

"Stop! I drowning! I no can breathe!" Tashi cried, but the men kept throwing seawater on him. Charley carried a big kettle from the galley and dumped more and more water on Tashi. It was madness!

At last the water stopped. John Hand came forward, brandishing the mop like Neptune's trident as a dripping Tashi sputtered and wiped water from his face. "Greetings from King Neptune," he said, bending from his waist in a mock bow. "You just crossed the equator, Tashi. You are the only one aboard who hasn't crossed the line before." Tashi soon found out that it was a tradition to be greeted by King Neptune. The sailors were all laughing. They came forward to shake hands and cuff Tashi on the ear. Soaked as he was, hair dripping, Tashi smiled and felt that he was truly part of the crew.

He rushed to the rail to look at the sea. It did not look any different than it had for days, but Tashi had crossed the equator and the ship was now in the Southern Hemisphere.

Dolphins were swimming alongside the ship. Tashi loved the dolphins and believed that they knew just what he was thinking. He felt that if he concentrated hard enough they would understand him. The dolphins were joining the celebration for the crossing of the equator, thought Tashi. Jumping and showing off for the ship was their way of saying congratulations.

After the excitement, Tashi leaned against the deckhouse, letting the sun and breeze dry his clothes. He planned to use the rest of the day to work on his model. He closed his eyes and relaxed, feeling the warmth of the sun on his face.

Shroosh. Shroosh. Odd sounds interrupted the calm that had just returned to the ship and made Tashi's eyes pop open.

"What's that noise?" asked Tashi. He scurried to the rail, expecting to see only the dancing dolphins. In the water, almost spitting distance from the *Sindia,* was a huge, gray shape spraying a cloud of vapor high into the air. *Shroosh. Shroosh.* Another cloud of vapor erupted from the shape.

"It's a whale, Tashi, and there's two more," said John Hand, pointing. "We often see them in the warm ocean." John and Tashi watched the huge creatures swim and dive, flopping their giant tails as they headed for the deep. John looked down at Tashi and chuckled, "King Neptune is giving you a real show!"

The barnacle-encrusted heads and bodies of the whales were so close that Tashi could feel and taste the salt water they splashed into the air. It was a thrilling display. "Thar she blows," whispered John as a whale blew another spray into the air. "That's how the whalers find the whales. They see the spouting and go get 'em," he said.

"We have whalers in Japan," said Tashi. "I don't think I want to kill one of those great beasts. They beautiful." The man and the boy stood at the rail until the whales disappeared. Tashi never took his eyes off the creatures, and John enjoyed watching Tashi discover and learn new things. Tashi had a quick mind; even his English was better than some of the sailors'.

It was a long voyage but never boring for Tashi. Each day was new and exciting. He would remember this day of seeing whales and crossing the equator forever. Sami would want to know everything, and Tashi had so much to tell. On days like this one, he missed his brother more than ever.

Chapter Six

Going Aloft

In Tashi's eyes the four masts of the *Sindia* seemed to tower to the sky. Each of the square-rigged masts had four to six sails, and the largest sails were bigger than Uncle's house. The wooden masts were bigger around than any tree in all of Kobe. Tashi could not begin to reach his arms around the base of these giant masts.

In his duties as a cabin boy, Tashi followed orders like the rest of the crew. They did what they were told when they were told. Their lives and the safety of the ship depended on the crew working together. No one man could sail this ship. It took ten men just to raise the sails. Each crew member knew his job.

Charley worked hard at his new chores in the galley. He had to do whatever Cookie asked and do it immediately, without comment. Cookie took advantage of Charley's help and never washed another dish.

"My hands is so raw from washing dishes that I'll never be able to hold the lines," grumbled Charley to the cook. "All the calluses is gone, and they ain't tough no more."

"Quit yer grousing, Charley," Cookie scolded, "and be glad yer in the kitchen where it's warm. Time'll come that you'll be glad to be in here. It's really cold rounding the Cape." Cookie handed Charley another pot to scrub.

Cooking on the *Sindia* was a haphazard event at best. The cook was in complete charge of the galley, and no one questioned his ways or what went into the food. Cookie only washed the pots with seawater when they were too dirty to use again, a practice which made Charley's scrubbing job a tough one. Besides washing dishes and cleaning up after Cookie, Charley sifted the bugs out of the flour and cut the maggots out of the meat.

Charley hoped that his time in the galley was just temporary. He was ambitious and wanted to learn about the other jobs on board. He wanted to be a good captain someday.

The *Sindia*'s sails had to be raised or furled by the crew. They raised the sails by winding the halyards around the huge capstan on the deck. This big wheel controlled the lines to raise the sails. When the wind was too strong and the sail area had to be reduced, all hands had to climb the rigging and tie down the sails by furling them to the spars. It was dangerous and complicated work.

"All hands on deck!" shouted George Wilkie. "We're in for a blow and have to shorten sail. Furl the topgallants and make fast!" Up the ratlines scrambled the crew.

Even before Wilkie stopped yelling, Charley had dashed from the cookhouse and climbed up the ratlines with the crew. He looked down at the deck so far below, felt the line bracing his feet and helped to furl the huge sail, singing a sea chantey that kept all of the men working in time.

They sang and they furled and then they climbed down the rigging. The ship was in tune again with the wind and the waves.

"How can they go up and not be afraid?" Tashi asked Wilkie as they watched the men.

"Going aloft is the test of being a real sailor," answered Wilkie. "You don't really understand until you've seen the sea from atop the mast."

"I go aloft someday," said Tashi firmly.

"You'll do it. You'll do it when you're told to," replied Wilkie. "It takes courage and someone ordering you up the first time. Ain't nobody would choose to hang on to a line a hundred feet over the middle of the ocean. You gotta be ordered to do it."

Not me, thought Tashi. I would go right now if no one would stop me. Being up in the sails as high as the gulls must be wonderful. I'll go up one day.

"Tashi, did you see me?" called Charley as he ran excitedly toward his friend. "I was on the foremast at the very end of the fore royal yard. We furled the sail in record time." Charley was very proud to be able to work with the men.

"I want go aloft, Charley," whispered Tashi.

The proud look on Charley's face faded. "Cabin boys don't do that," he said haughtily. As an apprentice in the galley, he was making his first trips aloft and was very protective of his status. Charley was happy to take charge of Tashi, but he wanted to make sure that Tashi knew his place on board.

"I want go aloft. If you won't help me, I find someone who will," muttered Tashi as he walked aft to the captain's quarters.

Charley watched Tashi march off and shook his head in disbelief. That rascal is really brave, he thought. Tashi never complained, never talked about missing his home and was ready to try anything, even going aloft. Charley had been so scared the first time he climbed the ratlines that his knees shook for a week. Of course, he had never let on to Tashi or Cookie that he had been frightened, but he was.

Tashi did his work and brought the captain a final mug of tea before bedding down for the night with dreams of climbing the rigging and watching the sea birds fly in their own space. He snuggled into the bedroll with Chauncey and thought about Sami and his family at home in Kobe. Every night when he went to bed, he missed his home. During the day he was too busy to think of anything but the ship and the voyage. As he drifted off to sleep with the cat purring on his chest, he dreamed about the Buddha hidden deep in the ship and felt at peace. Tashi prayed the Buddha would keep him and his family safe and would guide him home once the ship reached New York.

Days of sailing in the Pacific Ocean were perfect. Hour after hour the ship plowed steadily through the vast blue space. The crew liked sailing the Pacific and, to a man, had horror stories of rounding Cape Horn. Tales of ships hitting icebergs and waves of water as high as the yardarms crashing on deck were told with great bravado. Sailing a ship was hard work, and each sailor wanted everyone else to know just how hard.

Every afternoon, between lunch and teatime, Captain MacKenzie took a nap. All the sailors knew it and answered to George Stewart who was in charge. On one smooth sailing afternoon Stewart was smoking his pipe and lounging on the deck. Tashi had finished his chores and was leaning against the deckhouse, looking at the billowing sails. He knew that this was the perfect time to go aloft. He went to the cookhouse to find Charley. In the hot galley, Cookie was snoozing at the table with his head on his arms. Charley was up to his elbows in greasy water, scrubbing.

"I help," said Tashi, grabbing a rag. In no time the two boys had the gigantic pots scrubbed and dried.

"Thanks, Tashi. You're a good mate, " said Charley to his friend. "Sometimes this is an awful job," he grimaced, looking at the messy galley and Cookie. "Let's get out of here."

The two boys raced to the bow to watch the ship dig into the water. As always, the figurehead of the *Sindia* stared straight ahead. The boys leaned over the rail as the bow dipped and lifted in and out of the waves.

"I want to go aloft; now is time," Tashi announced to Charley. "The captain sleeping, Cookie, too. Stewart not watching. We go up mainmast to crow's nest."

"Do you know how many lashes we could get for doing this?" Charley tried to sound firm and in authority. As he spoke to Tashi, he was very careful not to look at him. He knew they were going aloft. He knew that Tashi would go with or without him, but he also knew that Tashi would be safer if he went along to talk him up the rigging and show him the way.

"The sailors know I go aloft. They say that they not see me," Tashi said stubbornly.

Charley sighed. "Well ... let's go," he said reluctantly.

The boys tried to act natural as they walked to the foredeck. The ratlines on the shrouds led straight up to the fore royal yards. Above them the crow's nest was empty. The wind was favorable, the sea calm and the ship was doing her best to keep the sailors happy. All sails were set and full. Climbing up behind the huge sails would make it possible for the boys to go unnoticed.

"I go first or you want first?" Tashi asked Charley.

"You go first. I'll be right behind you," Charley answered. They scrambled up the ratlines which formed a rope ladder in the shrouds.

Tashi looked over his shoulder and grinned. "This easy. We almost there."

"We're halfway to the first upper topsail. The second half is the longest. Don't look down; you'll get dizzy," Charley warned.

Tashi was setting a pace to make a captain proud. He hung on to the ratlines and placed his feet firmly on the rope ladder. He had chosen a good day. The ship was as steady as a sailing ship can be. Only the constant sway of the sea and the ever-present wind made the climb difficult.

Tashi never slowed. They reached the base of the crow's nest and crawled inside. Charley started to stand, but Tashi pulled him down. "No need ask for trouble. They not see us if we stay down. That good enough."

The truth was that Tashi could not stand. His knees were shaking and too weak to hold him. He was even a little dizzy looking down at the distant deck below them. The boys sat on the platform and looked out over the ocean.

The sea was many shades of blue. The ship was alone on the water.

"How see so far and not see other ship or land?" questioned Tashi. "How we know where we are going? It all the same on all sides of ship."

"The captain uses the stars at night and the sun in the day to fix where we are. He knows the position of the sun and the stars. He can tell by their position where we are. You have to be real smart to navigate a ship," replied Charley solemnly.

"We have much to learn," whispered Tashi. "Let's get below before we caught."

"Tashi, follow me. I'll go first," said Charley.

The boys climbed carefully down the ratlines and jumped from the rail to the deck. Suddenly they stopped short. There was John Hand, standing at the railing and watching them as he tamped tobacco into his pipe.

"Nice day, boys," John said, noting their surprised faces. "What's for dinner, Charley?"

"W- w- Wilkie caught some grouper, and we're going to eat it tonight," stammered Charley.

"Sounds good to me," muttered John through his teeth. He lit his pipe and walked aft to his workbench so the boys couldn't see the smile on his face.

Charley and Tashi looked at each other, knowing they were safe. They each ran off to work, Charley to the galley, Tashi to the chart house, without saying a word.

Chapter Seven

Southern Cross
and Albatross

Four bright stars shone in the deep blue night sky. Tashi joined Captain MacKenzie at the helm. The sky was clear, and the stars sparkled like diamonds in the dark. "See the cross in the heavens," the captain said, pointing up to the four stars.

Tashi looked and could see the pattern of a brilliant cross in the sky which stood out among all of the other stars.

"Those stars tell you that you are in the Southern Hemisphere and are approaching Cape Horn," mused the captain. "When you see the Southern Cross, you know that you're getting close to the tip of South America. Tomorrow we'll see the mountains."

Tashi liked the idea that Captain MacKenzie always knew where they were on this vast ocean. Each day now, Tashi watched him use the sextant to take a reading of the sun at the horizon to determine the ship's position in relation to the sun. Tashi did not quite understand the process but was beginning to get the idea.

"How many nautical miles circle the earth?" quizzed the captain.

"I not know, sir," answered Tashi.

"There's twenty-one thousand six hundred nautical miles. I have sailed around her more times than I can count." Captain MacKenzie was in a talkative mood. "We'll have to teach you about latitude and longitude. You seem to want to know everything. Let's see if you can master that tomorrow."

"Aye, aye, sir. I like that," replied a pleased Tashi.

Tashi knew that latitude and longitude were imaginary lines drawn on the globe. Longitudinal lines measured east and west from Greenwich, England, and circled through the North and South poles. Latitudinal lines circled around the earth north and south of the equator. On a chart, these lines helped navigators measure distance and find their position. Tashi did not let on that he even understood the words. He would let the captain explain.

That night Tashi pulled his bedroll out on the open deck under the stars. He would have to remember how they appeared in the dark sky. Sami could not see these stars in Japan. Tashi dreamed of putting the cross of stars in a bag, taking them to the street in front of his house and releasing them to his own familiar sky. He slept well, wrapped in his warm wool blanket with Drake.

In the morning Tashi woke to very different weather. The air was cold and grey. Overhead, albatross followed the ship. The crew was happy to see the albatross soaring over the *Sindia's* wake. These huge, white birds with a ten-foot wingspan were considered to be a good omen. They often followed ships for days, and some sailors thought that the birds were the spirits of lost seamen.

Charley grinned when he saw the birds. "We'll slide by

the Horn with the albatross leading the way," he said to Tashi as they watched the birds hover like white angels over the ship.

But Tashi was not interested in birds at the moment. "I have never been so cold," the small, shivering boy told Charley.

"It'll be colder than this at the Cape," Charley said firmly. "Guess I could give you the sweater that Granny knit me. It's way too small for me now."

"Can we get it now? I freezing," said Tashi.

As the boys went to the foc'sle to get the sweater, Tashi noticed that all the men were wearing oiled wool sweaters and caps to stay warm in the damp, chilly air.

As usual, Briggs was the only deck hand complaining about the cold. "If we'd left Kobe four weeks earlier, we wouldn't be freezin' now," he muttered as the boys walked by. The crew was tired of listening to Briggs. All of them would be happy to see him go ashore in New York.

"Land ho!" came the cry from the crow's nest. "Land ho! Off the port bow!" In the distance, the lookout could see the beginning of the land. It had been several months since the crew had seen anything but the ocean. The crew rushed to the rail, and the men squinted into the mist.

"Where are we?" Tashi demanded of John Hand who was

also trying to catch the first glimpse of shore.

"There they are," he explained, pointing as the mist parted. "Those are the mountains on the coast of Chile. We're approaching the entrance to the inland passage that takes you round the Horn. I've sailed this voyage several times, and each time is different and dangerous."

"What is this Horn like?" asked Tashi.

"It ain't nothing but a little bare island. Sailing by it gets you to the Atlantic Ocean, and it is some of the worst sailing there is. Even though it's summer down here, you might get to see an iceberg and you'll be cold, that's for sure. Be happy you're sleeping in the captain's quarters. It's cold and wet in the foc'sle when we round the Cape."

John had told Tashi the truth, but he hadn't told him everything. The carpenter knew that the passage around Cape Horn could be treacherous and frightening. At the Cape there would be giant waves called greybeards. Despite its steel hull, the ship would strain, and some of the greybeards would crash on the deck, wetting every sailor in the foc'sle. As Tashi peered into the fog, he was approaching one of the most difficult ship passages in the world.

Chapter Eight

Cape Horn

The sun had disappeared or so it seemed, leaving the *Sindia* surrounded by grey fog that penetrated the ship and the men aboard. Staying well off shore and heading south, the *Sindia* worked her way down the coast of Chile. The crew seldom glimpsed the mountains on the coast through the fog.

"Captain, have you set the course?" asked Wilkie as the ship plodded through a sea of dull water.

"We're going around," replied the captain. "It's summer here, and if the weather holds we can run outside and save time."

"Aye, Captain," replied the mate in his Scottish brogue, "'tis a hard passage no matter the course. It will be good to have a favoring wind on our back."

To Wilkie, this meant they were not taking the tedious and complicated inland passage through the Strait of Magellan. They were heading around the tip of South America on the open sea and entering the Atlantic Ocean through the Strait of le Maire. The captain was correct, Wilkie thought. Sailing from the west to the east with the prevailing wind was the easy way to round Cape Horn. If all went well, it would take about fifteen to twenty days to sail from fifty degrees latitude south on the Pacific to fifty degrees latitude south on the Atlantic. It would still be an adventure and would not really be easy.

While the captain plotted the *Sindia's* passage, Tashi was quickly learning how to stay warm and kept a watch for new birds and animals in this pewter-colored sea. The sight of the distant mountains comforted him, even if there were no plans to put into port.

Some of the crew kept busy sewing new sails and repairing old ones. High above the deck, other sailors checked the rigging for breaks and needed repairs. Everywhere on board, a feeling of tension and anticipation prevailed. It was a feeling that Tashi did not understand since he was the only person who had not sailed round Cape Horn.

"Look at that bird!" shouted Tashi as he pointed to a black bird soaring overhead. "It's the biggest bird I ever see! I hope it not land on deck!"

Charley heard Tashi's yells and rushed from the galley to see what was happening. John Hand stood at his bench near the galley door and envied their enthusiasm as the boys watched the huge birds skimming just above the masts, casting eerie shadows on the deck. Then John returned to shaping a new rail spindle. He knew that the next few days could be dangerous and his diligent repairs just might keep them safe.

"It's a condor, Tashi. It could probably fly away with you, you little runt," Charley said, disappointed that there was nothing more exciting than a bird to be seen.

"Beautiful and ugly at same time," mused Tashi as he observed the condors spiral higher into the sky. "No feathers on head. Strange. I wonder where it live?"

"I think that they live in the mountains and steal babies from their beds," replied Charley with a smirk on his lips.

"You telling me another story," said an indignant Tashi, but he held tight to the railing, just in case.

The boys were craning their necks to the sky when one of the sailors shouted, "School of turtles! Bring the harpoon!"

Tashi and Charley ran to the bow to see dozens and dozens of turtles swimming near the ship. The cluster of dark heads was almost invisible as the turtles bobbed up and down in the grey sea. As they neared the ship, Tashi could barely see their brown shells under the water.

"Charley, those turtles bigger than me!" Tashi was amazed at the size of the animals swimming toward the *Sindia.*

One of the seamen grabbed a harpoon, crawled out on the bowsprit and waited, his right arm held high in the air with the harpoon poised. In his left hand he held the line attached to the harpoon, ready to hold onto his catch. Another sailor shouted orders to the helmsman to keep the turtles in range. Captain MacKenzie liked turtle steak and turtle soup. The sailors knew that he would be pleased if they caught a big one.

As the ship sailed into the midst of the turtles, the sailor hurled the harpoon. He waited a second, peering into the water, and then he shook his fist triumphantly in the air. "Cookie, put the pot on! We've got ourselves a turtle!" he shouted.

Several sailors hauled the turtle aboard. "Glory! It must weigh ten stone," said Charley as he and Tashi watched. "That shell's over three feet long." The turtle's shell was covered with barnacles and slipper shells hitching a free ride.

Tashi and Charley were happy to have a change of menu. "We'll not have moldy meat for dinner tonight, Tashi," said Charley, licking his lips at the thought of the good meal to come.

"Well, boys, gonna make me work, are ye?" Cookie had arrived and was watching the floundering turtle on the deck. "Looks like we can eat for a week on that 'un. Good job, lads."

"What do you want me to do?" Charley asked.

"Go tell the cap'n we've got ourselves a big turtle. He'll want to be seein' it before we put it in the pot. Go on now." Cookie sent Charley off to get the captain.

Dinner was wonderful. Steaming turtle soup made the rainy, miserable day disappear, leaving the sailors drowsy and full.

❁　❁　❁

That night, the off-duty crew were sleeping warm in their bunks when Wilkie's urgent, "All hands on deck!" came down the foc'sle hatch. It landed with the sound of water breaking on the deck, a thunderous crash that nearly drowned out Wilkie's command. The men hurried above to a deck awash with seawater and battered by a frigid wind howling through the rigging.

"Furl the topgallants!" hollered Wilkie through the megaphone. Fifteen men climbed up the ratlines to the yards to shorten sail. The royals had been furled for days. Now the topgallants were coming down to prevent the wind from toppling the ship. These upper sails would overpower the ship in this heavy weather.

Furling the sails took several hours, and the sailors' numbed fingers bled from the hard work. Tashi watched from the protection of the deckhouse and wondered if he would ever be up to this kind of strength and service. He could see Charley hanging on for dear life but doing the job. He said a silent prayer to Buddha that the crew would all make it safely back to deck.

As the sailors descended the rigging, Captain MacKenzie shouted, "Watch on deck!" This command meant that every-one had to remain on deck no matter how tired or cold. It was the most inflexible of commands.

Tashi spent his time running between the galley and the wheel with mugs of hot tea and food for the officers. They worked tirelessly to keep the ship on course and safe. Ferocious winds screamed in from all directions, and the *Sindia* strained and groaned aloud as she fought her way through the rough seas.

Over the next few days, the calls of "Ice ahead to port!" or "Ice to starboard!" were heard often from the sharp-eyed lookout in the crow's nest. The helmsman responded to the cries, steering the ship to keep it from blundering into an iceberg. Chunks of ice, some half the size of the *Sindia*, floated everywhere in the water and presented a real hazard.

But the harsh weather and cold waters brought the bonus of new animals that delighted Tashi. "Look, there are the penguins!" exclaimed Captain MacKenzie one morning. Tashi, following closely on one of the captain's many errands, promptly ran to the rail and saw the graceful little animals slide down an ice floe into the water and launch themselves back on the iceberg to repeat their slide. On the ice, they marched like black-and-white soldiers on parade. Another tale to tell Sami, thought Tashi.

Like most of the crew, Tashi had been thrilled to see land again, but the bare mountains jutting into the clouds and the icy winds had Tashi remembering the warm, pleasant days sailing in the Pacific.

"Cape Horn to port!" came the cry from the lookout. Tashi could barely see a knobby island in the distance. That's it? he wondered in astonishment. That's the Cape Horn that everyone talks about?

A strong hand squeezed his shoulder. "Well, Tashi, there she is. You have just rounded the Cape. What do you think?" Tashi looked up to see Captain MacKenzie smiling for the first time in days.

"I thought it would be big island, and we would be closer to it."

"No need to be any closer. Just going around counts. Next we will see Staten Island and the Cape San Diego. Then we will be in the Atlantic Ocean and on to New York." Captain MacKenzie sounded pleased.

In a few days the *Sindia* passed through the Strait of le Maire and entered the Atlantic Ocean. It was another first for Tashi who was feeling like a real sailor having just rounded Cape Horn. John Hand helped him celebrate by telling him that his half model was finished and ready to be oiled. Tashi was pleased. He took the model for Cookie and Charley to admire.

"Hello, boy! What is that?" asked Cookie as he continued to pare a mountain of potatoes.

"It half model of *Sindia*," replied Tashi. "I work for long time to finish it."

Charley ran his hand over the smooth wood and whistled low. "Wish I could do that," he said with a little envy in his voice.

"I wish I could furl sails like Charley," Tashi said to his friend.

After their encounter with Cape Horn, all of the men on the ship relaxed. They talked of being in port and how they would spend their pay. This was the last stretch of a voyage that had been a good one.

Tashi had begun to check the position of the ship each morning and each evening. Captain MacKenzie had given his lesson on latitude and longitude, and Tashi wanted him to know that he appreciated his help. By November 12 the ship was five degrees south of the equator and thirty-three degrees west of Greenwich, England.

"Ship ahoy!" called the lookout. Tashi ran to the port rail and saw another four-master, sails full and heading south. He did not hear the ship identify itself, but he heard Wilkie's loud, clear voice answer through the megaphone, "Vessel *Sindia* bound for New York!"

The other vessel replied that it was bound for Cape Horn and San Francisco. Sighting another ship was an event for the sailors on the *Sindia* who had not once been ashore for more than four months. When Wilkie had shouted, "bound for New York," every man aboard knew that the voyage would soon end.

Chapter Nine

The Wreck

Tashi leaned against the side of the cookhouse and rubbed the third coat of tung oil onto the smooth mahogany of his model of the *Sindia*. A warm breeze ruffled his dark hair and gave a new motion to the ship. The Atlantic Ocean had a very different feeling than the Pacific. He noticed that the attitude of the crew had also changed from anxiety to anticipation as they sailed into the Atlantic.

Weather is so important on a sailing ship, and the weather in the Atlantic was a welcome change after sailing round Cape Horn. It was summer in the Southern Hemisphere, and the crewmen were glad to leave their woolen sweaters in the foc'sle and the ice of Cape Horn behind. Even when the *Sindia* hit the warm doldrums off the northern coast of South America, a place where the wind stopped and the ship almost stood still, the sailors went contentedly about their duties. They talked about the wonderful, cooling trade winds they would soon find as they approached the continent of North America. The trade winds would carry them through the beautiful, blue Caribbean Sea.

October and November were almost perfect sailing months in the Atlantic Ocean. Tashi had learned the names of all of the *Sindia's* many sails — topsails, gallants, royals, spanker — odd names that had now become familiar. Most of the time he knew which sails would be used in different wind conditions. The routine of the sea had become his life. He was part of the crew of this big ship, and now he only dreamed of Kobe and Sami once in a while.

When December arrived, the ship was off the coast of North Carolina. The sharp bite of winter was in the air and reminded Tashi of Cape Horn. Blustery winds with snow squalls made deck chores miserable. In the captain's quarters, Lee's cage swung to and fro as the *Sindia* plodded through the quartering seas.

"Look at these islands, Tashi," said Captain MacKenzie as he braced his feet and pointed to the Bermudas on the chart. "That's one of the prettiest places in the world. If you ever have the chance to go there on a ship, you go. I am sure you won't be sorry." Captain MacKenzie shifted the chart and pointed to another area west of the Bermudas. "This area off the coast of North Carolina called Diamond Shoals is known as the graveyard of the Atlantic. There are hundreds of wrecked ships in that area. We must be very careful. We don't want to run the *Sindia* aground as those other ships have done."

Tashi looked at the chart and easily traced the course he had sailed on the *Sindia*. When Captain MacKenzie plotted the day's progress, he always allowed Tashi to watch. The captain liked the boy's enthusiasm for navigation and encouraged his interest. Tashi still did not understand the use of the sextant, the instrument the captain used to fix the position of the sun, but he kept trying.

"Captain, how far New York?" asked Tashi.

"We are right on schedule and should be there in ten days, but if this awful weather holds up, I may have to change that answer."

As the *Sindia* made her way north, the air grew colder. Within days, the ship had passed both the Chesapeake and the Delaware bays and was off the coast of New Jersey. Weather in this part of the Atlantic Ocean in the month of December was unpredictable. On some days, the sky was a brilliant, hard blue. On other days, snow and rain squalls from dark clouds came blasting out of the northeast. Dressed in layers of borrowed clothing, Tashi braved the wind and the icy decks and carried mug after mug of hot tea to the officers at the helm.

By the middle of the month, the unsettled weather had worn down both the officers and the crew. On the night of the fourteenth, a very tired Tashi curled up in his little corner in the companionway. All day he had kept moving just to stay warm. The sun had been shining, but a cold curtain of snowy wind kept its warmth from reaching the ship. Tashi snuggled down in the warm blankets with Drake and put his arms around the dog's neck. Soon he was dreaming. In his dream, he and Sami were crew members on a big sailing ship, even bigger than the *Sindia*. Sami had learned to be a cook and ran the galley. Tashi was the captain and Charley was his first mate. This ship only sailed when it was warm and breezy and when the sky and the ocean were blue. The figurehead was a beautiful gold Buddha that announced to the oceans, "Keep this ship safe." It was a wonderful dream.

Suddenly, Tashi and Drake were slammed against the bulkhead of the captain's cabin. Drake started to howl, and a still-sleepy Tashi held him close, struggling to wake up and trying to comfort the frightened dog at the same time.

Crash! A deafening noise boomed in the companionway as one of the big spars fell on deck. The noise of the breaking spar and whipping sails scared Tashi, but worse yet was the stillness of the ship. The *Sindia* was not moving! Captain MacKenzie burst from his cabin, almost stepping on Tashi and the barking dog. Tashi scrambled out of his blankets and hurried from the protected companionway to the open deck with Drake close behind.

On deck, Tashi landed in a heap when he hit a patch of ice. The wind was howling and snow blew across the deck, stinging the men's faces like needles and coating the decks with a skim of ice. The sailors lost their footing and careened into one another as they rushed to control the foundering ship. Tashi was scared. So was everyone else.

George Stewart stood by the helmsman shouting, "Breakers ahead! Breakers ahead!" The boat rocked from side to side, but it was not moving forward.

Aground! thought Tashi. *We are aground!*

For the last six months Tashi had been listening and learning. He had heard all of the sailors say that running aground was the worst thing that could happen to a ship. Now, Tashi knew it had happened, and he went to find his best friend.

Getting to the cookhouse was not easy. Tashi found a dazed-looking Charlie clinging to the cookhouse doorway. As the two boys waited for orders, they scrabbled along the sloping deck, awash with sleet and seawater. They clutched the railing as they groped their way forward in the slush. "I see lights!" shouted Charlie in Tashi's ear. "See the lights over there?"

The lights must mean that we are close to shore, but where are we, wondered Tashi as he shivered in the blowing, frozen rain that hurt his face.

"Aground — we've run her aground," mumbled the sailors as they skidded on the slippery deck.

"Who was on watch?"

"What's the sounding?"

The questions went around as the sailors scrambled to their duties, trying to make fast the sails and await orders on what to do on the heaving ship.

"Signal the shore!" shouted Captain MacKenzie. "Get those lanterns lit! We have to know if someone ashore sees us. This is one terrible mess!" The captain grabbed the megaphone from Wilkie.

"Stewart! George Stewart!" he roared.

Everyone knew that the first mate was in for a real tirade from the captain. Earlier that night, Stewart had taken a sounding to measure the depth of the water. If the water had been deep enough, the sailors knew that the *Sindia* would not have grounded. Stewart must have made a mistake and not found the ship's proper position on the chart. The captain would want to know how this terrible thing had happened.

Wilkie ordered the crew to furl the blown-out sails to stop some of the deafening noises. Straining to hold onto the lines, part of the crew lowered the halyards while others tried to ascend the ratlines as the ship lurched with each battering wave. "Haul her down and make fast!" shouted Wilkie to several men near the stern. The men lowered the spanker and furled the sail, tying it tightly. The sails had to be secured to keep the ship from leaning and digging deeper into the sand.

The wind was blowing the *Sindia* closer to shore and harder aground, but no one could climb the icy ratlines to furl the square sails. Tashi watched, horrified, as one sailor after another slipped down the ice-encrusted rigging.

It was just after midnight when the ship grounded. Despite the panic, Captain MacKenzie had ordered some of the crew to their bunks to try to warm up and maybe get a little sleep. They would then be ready to spell the sailors working in the wicked cold. He knew that winter weather in the Atlantic often tested ships and their sailors. This night was beyond fierce.

Hoping to keep the listing ship upright, Captain MacKenzie called the order to set the anchor to windward. While the wind screeched and roared through the rigging and the ship rocked up and down, and back and forth, the men yelled at each other to be heard above the noise and created more confusion. In the pitchy blackness, Captain MacKenzie ordered Wilkie to launch the lifeboats in the hope of towing the ship to deeper water. The men lowered the first boat, but the wind tore it from its mooring, smashing it into the side of the *Sindia*. It hung midway between the rail and the water, useless. The *Sindia* was hard aground.

Belowdecks, the cargo lashings held, and the barrels of pottery and other crates stayed in place. Some of the casks of camphor oil had broken open, and the biting, medicinal scent filled the hold and foc'sle. Tashi said a quick prayer to Buddha for rescue; he remembered the statue and hoped it was safe.

Once the cargo was checked, Captain MacKenzie ordered all hands on deck to fasten any loose equipment to the ship and to prepare to be rescued. He knew there was no hope of floating the ship tonight.

"Light the flares and fire the rockets!" commanded the captain.

The sky turned red-orange in the light of the flares. In the brief afterglow, Tashi could see the breakers slosh over the deck and continue in to the shore where shapes of houses were just visible. He squinted at the distant beach and could see a few lighted windows but could not make out any signs of life. The sailors could only hope that their signals had been seen ashore.

Chapter Ten

On the Beach

"**M**y feets so cold I can't even feel 'em," grumbled Ed Boyd as he headed up the beach from Middle Station. The United States Life-Saving Service at Thirty-sixth Street was almost in the middle of the narrow, sandy barrier island that it sat upon. Wish I hadn't drunk so much cider, thought Boyd as he hunched his shoulders, hitched up his pants and headed into the wind. Should be meeting up with Harry soon.

At the same moment, Harry Young was heading south from the Fourth Street Life-Saving Station located at the island's north end. Lifesavers all up and down the coast were out in this terrible storm, making their routine inspections of the beaches and scanning the sea for vessels in trouble. It was the custom for the lifesavers to exchange brass tokens as they met on their routes, proof that the men had completed their inspection. Harry Young would meet Ed Boyd; they would exchange tokens, then turn around and walk back to their stations in the cold, sleety darkness.

Through the swirling snow and sand, Young saw the ghostly figure of Boyd emerge. "What's that?" he shouted into the wind as the men met. Through the yowling wind and snow, he could hear abandoned sails cracking like distant pistol shots. A longtime sailor, Harry Young knew there was trouble.

"Terr'ble night," Boyd answered. "Trouble never happens in the summer, just when it's too cold to think. Let's go!"

The two men, heads lowered to avoid the prickling snow, made their way down the beach. Through the blowing sand and snow, they saw the faint light of the *Sindia's* lanterns and the rockets flying in the air.

"I can see the masts. She's a big 'un," muttered Young as the full silhouette of the foundering ship appeared in the distance. "Can't do anything until morning," he said, as Boyd nodded his agreement. "Let's signal with the Coston lights and let 'em know we've seen 'em."

Young shot a red flare. Within a minute, the ship signaled back. Boyd stayed on the beach and gathered driftwood to build a fire to keep warm and to let the sailors know that someone was watching out for them. Young pulled up his coat collar and hunched into the wind, making his way back to the Fourth Street Station to inform Captain Mackey Corson about the ship.

When Young entered the station house, he was surprised to see everyone up. The lifesavers had roused themselves out of warm beds, and Captain Corson was buttoning up his coat, preparing to go to the beach to appraise the situation.

"Is she a big 'un?" he asked. "People from downbeach have been tellin' us that the racket from the busted sails woke 'em up. How far off the beach is she?"

"We could see the ship 'bout three hundred feet off the Sixteenth Street beach. She's got four masts. They didn't get all the sails down in this howl. Doesn't look good." Harry Young was talking and shucking off his wet, cold slicker as the rest of the men put on theirs.

"Can we get the breeches buoy out there?"

"She's rockin' pretty bad. Don't know if it'll hold," replied Young as he reached for a dry slicker hanging nearby.

"Well, we'll try it. Take the breeches buoy," ordered Captain Corson.

The word-of-mouth grapevine was working. By the time the lifesavers had hauled the breeches buoy to the Sixteenth Street beach, Captain A.C. Townsend and his crew from Middle Station had already joined Boyd at his bonfire with the station's surf boat. The *Sindia* listed at a sharper angle now. As the storm waves raced toward the beach, they smacked into the ship, settling it deeper into the sand.

"Well, A.C., she's not going anywhere today," remarked Mackey Corson wryly. "That ship is hard aground." The *Sindia's* bow pointed south, and the whole ship listed to the port side, making it hard for the lifesavers to see how many men were aboard.

"Guess we have to try to set up the breeches buoy. Don't want to oar in that sea, Mackey."

Captain Corson nodded in agreement. The two men had worked together as lifesavers for a long time and had seen other ships run aground on this beach. "Besides," said Townsend, "she 'pears to have a steel hull. Don't need to worry 'bout her breakin' up."

"Set her up!" ordered Corson.

The two crews went to work constructing a big, wooden, x-shaped frame for the breeches buoy. The plan was to shoot a line through the frame to the ship, where the sailors would make fast the line to the mast. The foundering ship would then be attached to the rescuers ashore and could haul a hawser from the beach to the ship. Strung on this heavy rope were a pulley and a ring buoy with a pair of pantslike breeches attached that a seaman could step into and ride ashore through the storm and the waves. Back and forth the breeches buoy would go. The lifesavers would send the buoy and pull the seamen ashore one at a time, a long, cold process in this coastal storm.

The lifesavers dug away snow and sand to set up and anchor the frame. It had to hold a line long enough to reach the ship and strong enough to carry a man's weight. By eight in the morning, under a dull, leaden sky, a loud charge of the Lyle gun sent a line flying toward the ship.

Chapter Eleven

The Rescue

Aboard the *Sindia*, it had been a long, exhausting night. With ice slicking the rigging, the crew had to climb down from the ratlines and leave the topsails unfurled. After losing one lifeboat to the wind, Captain MacKenzie ordered the crew to lash all loose lines and equipment on deck and start the pumps to clear the bilges. It was a hopeless task.

Tashi confined Chauncey and Drake to the captain's cabin. The two animals were terrified, whining and scratching at the cabin door. Swinging in his cage, Lee made a racket that was lost in the din of flapping sails and crashing sea.

Captain MacKenzie, followed closely by George Stewart, came into the cabin. "Keep those animals out of the way!" he bellowed at Tashi.

He turned to Stewart. "Now, show me where you think we are. What was your sounding?" His voice was carefully controlled.

"Thirty-six fathoms, sir. I – I thought we were right here," he stammered, pointing to the entrance to New York Harbor.

"Well, it can't be. We're hard aground. How many readings did you take?" As Stewart opened his mouth to answer, the captain snapped, "Not enough, you fool!"

Just then the *Sindia* lurched to port and the charts slid off the navigation table into a useless heap. Tashi sat on the floor comforting Drake and Chauncey as the captain and Stewart went out on deck. Tashi quickly followed but went to the cookhouse to find Charley.

Cookie was bashing the pots back onto the stove and cursing everyone and everything. He was standing ankle-deep in water that had spilled from the pots and through the cookhouse door. His precious soup was on the deck in clumps of sodden cabbage and potatoes.

"Come on, Tashi. Let's get out of here," said Charley. He grabbed Tashi's arm and they waded out to the deck and climbed to the top of the cookhouse.

Flat on their stomachs and gripping the seam of the sloping roof, the boys could see the shore just over the rail of the listing ship. Overhead, shredded sails cracked and flapped in the wind. In the morning light the boys watched the lifesavers set up the breeches buoy. As Charley explained the procedure to Tashi, the Lyle gun fired. The line fell into the water.

"Shoot! Shoot!" Charley hoarsely urged the lifesavers. "Got it!" he shouted as a seaman grabbed a line which landed on the deck.

The sailors fastened the line to the mast, and then they hauled the breeches buoy and pulley aboard. Captain Mac-Kenzie ordered a reluctant Briggs into the breeches, and two seamen hoisted him over the side of the ship for his ride to shore. He was going smoothly across the waves when the ship lurched again, sending both Briggs and the line into the water. When he surfaced, still attached to the ship, they hauled him back, dripping and cursing with cold and fright.

"Not going to work," Charley said dejectedly. He and Tashi stayed on the roof where they could see all of the action.

"What to do?" Tashi asked his friend.

"They'll have to row out in their lifeboat. It'll be a cold, wet ride, but they'll have to come."

"What on shore?" questioned Tashi.

"They'll feed us and we'll dry out. We'll have to find another ship. This 'un's a goner!" Charley was pretending to know everything. "You stay with me, Tashi. We're true mates."

"Boat coming!" Tashi had not taken his eyes off the beach where a crowd of people had braved the weather and gathered to watch the *Sindia*. Tashi could see the lifeboat that had been launched in the surf and was on its way. Up and down over the rolling waves the little boat approached.

The boys slid down from the roof and joined the other sailors at the taffrail to watch the bobbing boat.

"Ocean City, New Jersey. So *that's* where we are," Charley said, reading the stenciled letters on the lifeboat's bow.

One of the seamen threw a line to a lifesaver, and Captain MacKenzie ordered eight men to board the little boat. Hand over hand, the sailors went down the line hung over the taffrail. Tashi ran to the cabin, wrapped Lee's birdcage in a sheet and hurried back to the taffrail. Tying the cage to a line, he lowered it carefully over the rail to Briggs, settled in the boat below.

Grudgingly, Briggs took the cage grumbling, "Captain cares more fer this tweeter than the crew."

Charley and Tashi watched the lifesavers struggle to return to shore. As the rowers went over the breakers, the little boat almost stood on end. Finally, the sailors climbed out on the beach and the lifesavers turned the boat around, returning to the *Sindia* for the next group. Tashi and Charley were ready to go with Drake and Chauncey. John Hand rigged rope harnesses to lower the cat and dog over the side. Tashi crawled over the taffrail and inched his way down the heavy rope to the waiting surf boat that rose and fell with each surging wave. Charley followed. John lowered the whimpering animals to the boys, and they headed for the beach.

In three trips all of the crew but the officers, Cookie and John Hand went ashore. Captain MacKenzie went with the crew on the last trip. He had to notify the *Sindia's* owners in New York of the wreck and ask for a tug to tow the ship. Later that evening, he returned to his damaged ship and his officers.

Chapter Twelve

Safe Harbor

Pointing and chattering, women in long skirts billowing in the cold wind, children in their Sunday finest and men with spyglasses focused on the *Sindia* stood in a row on a boardwalk. Tashi, cradling Chauncey in his arms, could hardly believe his eyes. A boardwalk by the sea was a new sight for him. He waded through the sea foam on the beach where the lifeboat had unloaded and followed the lifesavers ashore. Charley trailed behind, tugging a reluctant Drake after him.

"Tashi! Tashi! Wait for us!" called Charley as he dragged the dog up the beach.

"Come on, boys!" A lifesaver, a husky man covered head to toe in his yellow sou'wester, gestured to Tashi and Charley. "We've got warm clothes and hot food waitin' at the station for us. Let's go." Harry Young had been out in the bad weather since the middle of the night. He wanted to get some dry clothes and rest.

Tashi stopped to wait for Charley and looked out at the sad ship. *Sindia's* proud figurehead was askew. Now the maharaja stared in the direction from which they had come as the ship listed more and more to port on the battering east wind. The water was not very deep, and the load line painted on the ship's hull was exposed at low tide to the fury of the wind and waves. Tashi took comfort from the warm cat in his arms as he viewed the ship.

"We're goin' to have to find ourselves another ship if we want to leave this place," said Charley as he caught up to his friend. "That ship ain't goin' nowhere!"

"Gotta step lively, boys," chided Young. "I've got work to do."

Charley and Tashi followed him through the dunes to the lifesaving station. By the time they had changed their clothes, eaten their fill of baked sweet potatoes, and dried off the cat and dog, the last boatload of sailors straggled in the door.

One of the sailors told the boys, "There's fourteen feet of water in the hold. It's real bad. The water comes in faster than the pumps can get it out! Cap'n says that a tug from New York will be here tomorrow, but I don't think they can break her loose." He opened his ditty bag and pulled out Tashi's half model. "Here's yer boat, Tashi. John Hand told me to give it to you."

Tashi smiled and reached for the *Sindia*. In his hurry to get the animals and himself off the sinking ship, he had forgotten his precious model. "Thanks."

He placed the small ship by the cat, curled up in the bottom of a lifeboat hauled out for the winter. Around him, other crew members gratefully took the warm blankets and bedded down on the floor in the midst of all the boats and equipment stored for the winter in the Ocean City Life-Saving Station.

As they left the station on Monday morning, the crew presented a colorful appearance dressed in assorted clothing provided by the Ocean City townsfolk. The men wandered down Asbury Avenue, the main street, looking for a pub. Most of the crew were from Great Britain and were used to spending their onshore time in the pubs, spinning yarns and swapping tales about their adventures at sea. There were no pubs in Ocean City.

"Guess I'll go watch for the tug," complained Briggs. "No pubs. Gotta leave this place." For once, Briggs' grumpy sentiment was shared by the rest of the crew.

Tashi and Charley were more interested in the *Sindia* than in finding a pub and had headed directly to the beach. By noon the tug arrived and fastened big hawsers to the ship to pull her off the sand bar at high tide. To lighten the ship, Captain MacKenzie ordered some of the cargo scuttled. Tatsumi mats and casks emptied of camphor oil floated ashore and littered the beach where the townspeople hauled away the cargo in wagons.

"Tug's got her," said Charley dejectedly as the boys watched from the boardwalk. Suddenly, he grabbed Tashi's shoulder and pointed to the ship. "Look at that! She's broke in two!" he exclaimed as a crack appeared in the hull, then widened to a split.

As the water rushed into the ship, Tashi pictured it rising in the hold. He felt certain that the statue of Buddha, hidden deep within the cargo, would now be safely buried in the sand.

Captain Corson ordered a surf boat to the *Sindia*. Tashi and Charley watched the officers, Cookie and John Hand climb down the rope and into the little boat. Captain MacKenzie was still on board, his back to the taffrail. As the boys watched, he hesitated, took off his cap, looked up at the streamers of torn sails, put on his cap, and went over the rail and down the rope.

Tashi and Charley stood on the beach and watched the lifeboat with Captain MacKenzie row to shore. Yesterday's raging surf had flattened into a smooth mirror of shining sea. The sun sparkled on the water and warmed the boys as Drake ran up and down the beach. Tashi knew that this sun was not shining on Kobe. His home was exactly halfway around the world. At this moment, it was dark there, and Sami would be sleeping.

Tashi's first sailing adventure was over. Tomorrow, Tashi and Charley and the other crew members would take the train from Ocean City to New York City. There Tashi hoped to find another ship to take him and his stories the rest of the way home.

Rigging of a Four-Masted Bark

1. Foremast
2. Mainmast
3. Mizzen mast
4. Jigger mast
5. Upper topsail
6. Lower topsail
7. Upper topgallant
8. Lower topgallant
9. Royal

10. Mainsail (Main course)
11. Foresail (Fore course)
12. Crossjack (Mizzen course)
13. Spanker
14. Gaff topsail
15. Staysails
16. Jibs
17. Ratlines
18. Bowsprit

Glossary

aft — *toward or at the stern on a boat or ship.*

bark — *a sailing ship with three to five masts, all square-rigged except the after mast which is fore-and-aft-rigged.*

bow — *the most forward part of a boat or ship.*

breeches buoy — *a life buoy with a canvas sling or "breeches" attached used for sea rescue. The buoy was suspended from a line between a shipwreck and the shore or another vessel. Shipwreck victims stepped into the buoy and were pulled to safety.*

bridge — *area on a ship where the wheel is located.*

camphor — *substance taken from a camphor tree and used as an ingredient in insect repellents and medicinal preparations.*

capstan — *a cylinderlike apparatus rotated manually; used in winding lines to hoist the sails and spars.*

companionway — *stair or ladder leading belowdecks; also a hallway between cabins.*

Coston light — *signal light.*

crow's nest — *a platform high on the main mast for a lookout.*

deckhouse — *structure built on the deck of the ship.*

embark — *to board a ship or start a voyage.*

foc'sle — *forecastle; a structure at the bow of the ship where the crew are housed.*

fore — *toward or at the bow of a boat or ship; prefix indicating this location, i.e. foredeck.*

furl — *to roll up and secure a sail by tying it to a yard.*

galley — *kitchen on a ship.*

half model — *accurate carving of the profile of a ship; can be mounted to a plaque.*

halyard — *rope that hoists the sail and keeps it up.*

hatch — *an opening in the deck of a ship; also, the cover or door for such an opening.*

hawser — *very heavy rope.*

helm — *a ship's steering wheel or tiller.*

hold — *space belowdecks where cargo is stored.*

list — *(of a ship or boat) to lean to one side or another.*

Lyle gun — *gun used by lifesavers to shoot a rope to a ship or target.*

marlinspike — *a pointed tool used to pry open knots and to separate strands in a rope.*

mast — *a wooden pole on which sails are set.*

port — *the left-hand side of a ship or boat, facing forward; often marked with a red light.*

ratlines — *small ropes fastened to the shrouds and forming a ladder for going aloft.*

rigging — *gear used to support and adjust the sails; includes the mast and halyards.*

sextant — *navigational instrument used to determine latitude and longitude by measuring the altitude of the sun, moon and stars.*

shoal — *sandbank or sand bar, especially one near an ocean beach that is exposed at low tide.*

shrouds — *wires stretched from the deck to the top of the mast to support the mast.*

sound — *measure the depth of the water.*

spanker — *triangular-shaped sail set on the aftermost mast of a sailing ship.*

starboard — *the right-hand side of a ship or boat facing forward; often marked with a green light.*

stern — *back end of a ship.*

taffrail — *railing above the stern of a ship.*

topgallants — *topmost square sails.*

watch — *period of time, usually four hours, when part of a ship's crew is on duty.*

yard — *a spar or tapered pole hung at right angles to the mast to support the head of a square sail.*

Fiction and Fact

This is a fictional account of a real event. The true story begins in Belfast, Ireland, in 1887 at the shipyard of Harland and Wolff where the *Sindia* was built. Three hundred twenty-nine feet long with a forty-five-foot beam and a draft of twenty-seven feet, this steel-hulled ship was fitted with the rigging of a four-masted bark and was reputed to be the largest and fastest sailing vessel afloat. From her bow projected a massive figurehead of a mustachioed man with a tricornered turban. The carving is believed to be the Maharaja Mahadji (1750-1795), a powerful ruler of the Scindia dynasty of India.

In 1900, American oil magnate John D. Rockefeller bought the *Sindia*, valued at $200,000, for his Standard Oil Company. What would be the ship's final voyage began in Bayonne, New Jersey, where the vessel was loaded with a cargo of case oil bound for China. After completing this leg of the voyage, she sailed from Shanghai to Kobe, Japan, where she picked up cargo for the return trip to New York, via Cape Horn.

The ship's manifest, or cargo list, included matting, manganese ore, Oriental curios and fine china, linseed, wax, camphor oil, and ornamental screens which were popular home decorations in the Victorian era. Through the years, rumors about "other cargo" have become part of the *Sindia* story. Legend has it that crewmen smuggled aboard a gold statue of Buddha, stolen from a shrine. With an uprising raging in China, a great deal of smuggling of valuable art and religious statues did occur. However, supposition is not always fact, and there is no evidence that the *Sindia* was engaged in smuggling.

Allan MacKenzie served as the *Sindia's* captain, logging more than 200,000 miles on the ship. A document at the Ocean City Historical Museum, in New Jersey, says the Scotsman's knowledge of the ocean achieved near-mythic proportions among sailors. "His face shrouded in heavy white whiskers typical of the old salts of clipper days and roving all the seas that are for thirty-five years, MacKenzie had become a tradition of the sea. In haunts of seamen it was said that 'His satanic majesty never sent a gale that did not turn in favor of MacKenzie.'"

On July 8, 1901, the *Sindia* cast off from the Kobe waterfront with a full hold and a crew of thirty-three, all English except for the Japanese cabin boy. The trip across the Pacific Ocean and around Cape Horn was uneventful. As the *Sindia* approached the coast of New Jersey, however, a winter coastal storm — a nor'easter — was gathering strength. Shortly after midnight on December 15, the ship ran aground on a sand bar in the howling snowstorm, settling about three hundred feet off the Sixteenth Street beach in Ocean City.

A few hours later, Harry Young and Edward Boyd, members of the U.S. Life-Saving Service, were out on beach patrol when they spotted distress signals from the stranded bark through the crashing surf and swirling snow. After signaling back with flares, the men notified the lifesaving stations at Fourth Street and at Thirty-sixth Street for rescue equipment.

When the equipment arrived, the lifesavers from the Peck's Beach station at Fourth Street shot a line to the battered ship, hoping to pull the crew across, one by one, in a pantslike sling called a breeches buoy. When that attempt failed, the lifesavers waited until daybreak and used a surf boat to bring the crew and their gear ashore. Captain MacKenzie and his six officers stayed on board and did not abandon the *Sindia* until the seventeenth. At that time, a tugboat from New York was

The Sindia, hard aground on the beach at Ocean City, New Jersey, a few days after the December 15, 1901 wreck. Visible in the distance, between the center masts, is a tugboat which unsuccessfully attempted to free the grounded bark.

unable to free her from the ten feet of sand in which her keel was buried.

Soon after the shipwreck, the Admiralty Court of King Edward VII held a hearing in Philadelphia to fix blame for the loss. According to a report issued by the London Board of Trade on February 7, 1902, "Allan MacKenzie ... failed to exercise proper and seamanlike care and precaution on approaching the land on the night of the 14th, and the morning of the 15th of December, 1901." This same report concluded that there was too much sail up and that not enough soundings were taken for the poor weather conditions.

Captain MacKenzie's master's certificate was suspended for six months. He died within the year, some said from the disgrace he believed that he had brought on his family.

George Stewart, the first mate who took the soundings and was on duty at the time of the wreck, was suspended for three months. Second Mate George Wilkie was cleared of any wrongdoing as was the crew; all received their proper wages.

After the wreck, ordinary seaman David Jackson remained in Philadelphia and became a United States citizen. In 1970, Jackson visited the Ocean City Historical Museum to reminisce about the voyage. He recounted how George Stewart mistook a light in Ocean City for "Highland Light," probably a reference to the Twin Lights at Atlantic Highlands, located at the entrance of New York Harbor. On many occasions, Jackson denied a popular rumor that the whole crew was intoxicated. He also confirmed that all members of the crew survived the wreck, as did Captain MacKenzie's cat, dog and canary.

In 1936 another survivor, J. Morley of Rugeley Staffs, England, corresponded with Captain Christopher Bentham of Coast Guard Station Ocean City and credited the Life-Saving Service with the rescue. (The U.S. Life-Saving Service was the forerunner of today's Coast Guard.) Harry Young and Ed Boyd were acknowledged to be the first surfmen to spot the wreck

Photographs from the book Peck's Beach/Down The Shore Publishing/collection of Ocean City Historical Museum

The Peck's Beach Life-Saving Station, with a surf boat being hauled out. From this station, crew members responded to the wreck of the Sindia.

which was reported to Captain Mackey Corson of Peck's Beach Station and to Captain A.C. Townsend of Middle Station. Others who participated in the rescue were Ed Boyd, Lewis Corson, Townsend Godfrey, Mulford Jeffries, Ralph Jones and Joseph Norcum. All of these names still appear in the Ocean City phone book, descendants of the surfmen of the Life-Saving Service.

As for the fabled statue and the *Sindia's* real cargo, an account in the Ocean City museum notes, "Some have whispered the idol was unwilling to be lodged among strange gods and unbelieving people and so decided to rest forever

Captain Mackey Corson of the Peck's Beach Life-Saving Station, center, stands with his crew of the U.S. Lifesaving Service.

beneath the silent sand." But other Ocean City residents found treasures for the taking or tried to wring a profit from the ship's sad end. Wrote Norman V. Sargent:

Every boy in Ocean City had a bamboo jumping pole, and some enterprising householders had bamboo fences. Many a floor was covered with slightly water-stained matting from the 24,747 rolls carried by the ship. In a hundred Ocean City homes today are bases or bits of bric-a-brac from the Sindia's *hold. For several years, camphor and eucalyptus oil were sold locally as "Sindia Oil," a panacea for everything from earaches to fallen arches.*

An attempt was made to salvage the valuable cargo of the Sindia, *and Customs officers were placed in a temporary "Custom House" built on the beach, where duty was collected on all the goods brought ashore. A group of local men bought the ship and cargo from representatives of the owners and insurance companies, getting for a song ($5,500), it was said, what had been valued at half a million dollars. The local men sold their prize to Mr. L.L. Eavenson, of the Evanson Naptha Borax Co., who had been told the ship could be floated, and learned later the cost would be prohibitive and the effort probably futile. At one time a pier was built to the vessel and an admission fee charged.*

A "Sindia Store" was opened on the Boardwalk, and the two large jardinieres on the platform of the Tabernacle, on Wesley Avenue between Fifth and Sixth Streets, were among the articles taken from the ship and sold there. This venture was also unprofitable because of the expense involved in employing divers and hoisting equipment to remove the cargo and convey it to shore. It is estimated that about one-fourth of the cargo is still in the vessel's hold, deep in the sand.

Today, the wreck of the *Sindia* is still part of Ocean City's heritage. In the Ocean City Historical Museum at 1735 Simpson Avenue, you can see the half model of the ship with its brass plaque reading "Carved by the Japanese Cabin Boy." Many pieces of Japanese porcelain recovered from the wreck are on display as is the stern-looking maharajah figurehead. Also on display is a five-foot model of the ship carved by Tom Adams of Linwood, New Jersey. Mr. Adams used the plans of the *Holkar*, a "sister ship" of the *Sindia* also built by Harland and Wolff.

On the northeast corner of Fourth Street and Atlantic Avenue stands the old Peck's Beach Life-Saving Station, now a private home. At 1636 Asbury Avenue is the Lake house where young Marion Lake woke to the noise of the blown-out sails and cracking spars of the beached *Sindia* on that fateful morning. At the museum, you can hear Marion, a cousin of Ocean City's founding family, tell her story on audio tape. Captain Mackey Corson's home is located at 420 Ocean Avenue.

Over the years, storms and beach restoration projects alternately uncovered and buried the *Sindia's* rudder post, at times visible from the Sixteenth Street boardwalk. In December of 1992, a huge winter storm washed away newly pumped-in sand, again exposing the rudder post. This piece of the *Sindia* was yanked from its intertidal home by a construction worker with a backhoe. Ocean City now has this remnant in storage.

Should you wish to walk the decks of a ship like the *Sindia,* there is a four-masted bark, *Peking,* on display at the South Street Seaport Museum in New York City.

L.C.H., January 1995

The author, Lucinda Hathaway, stands with the rudder post of the
Sindia *on the beach in Ocean City, New Jersey, shortly before this last*
visible piece of the shipwreck was removed and put in storage by the city.

About the Author

For twenty-five years, Lucinda Hathaway has lived on Peck's Beach in Ocean City, New Jersey. Raised in landlocked West Virginia, she now divides her time between Ocean City and another island, in the Gulf of Mexico. She is the founder and director of Ocean City's "Beachwalk," an environmental education project that has involved more than twelve thousand participants through the project's forty dedicated volunteers. It is perhaps more than coincidental that her birthday is July 8, the same date the *Sindia* sailed from Kobe, Japan, on her fateful voyage. *Takashi's Voyage* is her first book.

Lucinda's husband, Jack, and her two daughters, Nancy and Diane, share her love of the sea.

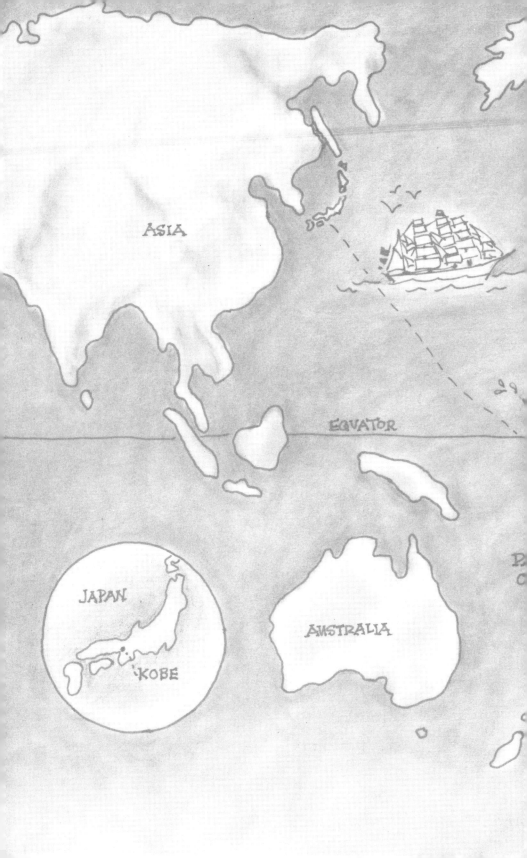